Dear Nurse

True Stories of Strength, Kindness and Skill

RCN Foundation
Illustrated by Michael Foreman

SCHOLASTIC

*The RCN Foundation would like to thank Jane Cantrell
and Sian Thomas for their support and guidance.*

50p from the sale of this book will be paid to the RCN
Foundation, of which 90% (45p) will be a donation to the
Foundation and 10% (5p) will be a licensing fee for the use of the RCN Foundation's
name and logo.

Published in the UK by Scholastic, 2023
1 London Bridge, London, SE1 9BG
Scholastic Ireland, 89E Lagan Road, Dublin Industrial Estate, Glasnevin, Dublin, D11 HP5F

Contributions by Elizabeth Mathai Varughese, May Richell Parsons, Kate O'Hagan,
Layla Lavallee, Karl Monaghan, Professor Alex McMahon, Jody-Ann Gordon, Margaret
Bayley, Rohit Sagoo, Lucy Bradford, Asha Parmar, Jessica Davidson, Victoria Jackson,
Hephzibah Samuel, Aisha Holloway, Maritess Murdoch, Suman Shrestha, Dame Janet
Elizabeth Murray Kershaw DBE FRCN, Simon Newman, Natalie Pattison, Nichole McIntosh,
Janette Streeting, Claire Roche, Cecilia Anim, Linsu Boniface, Victoria White, Jacqui Tahari,
Jessica Anne Filoteo, Nicola Ring, Hannah Grace Deller, Carlito Adan, Julia Terry, Femke
Steffensen, Jade Stewart, Francesca Steyn, Laura Jayne Simms, Karen Jephson,
Dame Anne Marie Rafferty, Deborah Sturdy, Dr Lissette Aviles, Sara Dalby, Sharon White.
Contributors © 2023.

Illustrations © Michael Foreman, 2023
Foreword © Jo Whiley, 2023
Introduction by Christie Watson © RCN Foundation, 2023

ISBN 978 07023 1714 9

Printed and bound in Italy by L.E.G.O S.p.A
Paper made from wood grown in sustainable forests and other controlled sources.

1 3 5 7 9 10 8 6 4 2

www.scholastic.co.uk

Any website addresses listed in the book are correct at the time of going to print.
However, please be aware that online content is subject to change and websites can
contain or offer content that is unsuitable for children. We advise all children be
supervised when using the internet.

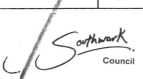 

Contents

Foreword

Jo Whiley

I'm incredibly proud to introduce to you this wonderful book celebrating the inspirational and vital work of nurses and midwives across the country.

The NHS has cared for me since the day I was born. Like many of us, I owe my life to the essential skills of nurses and midwives, the cornerstone of our NHS.

Every year of my life has been marked by visits to hospitals, sometimes for myself, sometimes for friends and family. When I was three, I had a major heart operation at Great Ormond Street Hospital. The care I received there, when only a baby, began my lifelong appreciation of nurses. My appreciation of our midwives came later when they helped deliver my four wonderful children.

During the pandemic, we all learnt to admire the work of nurses and midwives that little bit more. My sister, Frances, who has a learning disability and complex needs, became very poorly with Covid. It is due to the talent of those caring for her in the hospital that Frances is with us today. The nurses of the NHS played a huge part in her treatment and recovery. I can never say thank you enough.

The stories in this book are from real nurses and midwives. When you read them, you'll see that there are many different jobs you can do within nursing. You'll see the huge difference these people make. From working with children to old people, in prisons, in care homes, or in the local doctor's surgery, there are countless ways that nurses and midwives help to keep us all healthy and well.

These stories are special because the people who wrote them are special. I hope that they will inspire you to think about becoming a nurse or midwife too.

Introduction

Christie Watson – *Patron, RCN Foundation, former nurse and best-selling author*

The RCN Foundation is immensely proud to present this collection of incredible stories about nursing and midwifery staff who work all across the country to look after people when they are unwell.

As you read this book, you will find nurses, midwives and healthcare support workers working in many different places, including hospitals, schools and even in people's homes. The RCN Foundation is here to help all nurses, midwives and healthcare support workers across the UK – sometimes nurses and midwives might need extra support if they are having a tough time. It also assists them in learning new skills to help them to further help patients and their families, friends and neighbours. People like you and me.

I am the Patron of the RCN Foundation, and I used to work as a nurse, so I know just how rewarding working within the nursing and midwifery professions can be. We hope that you will enjoy reading the stories of these amazing people, and that you might even be inspired to follow in their footsteps one day.

You can find out more about the RCN Foundation by going to the website: www.rcnfoundation.org.uk

Healing Words

Elizabeth Mathai Varughese,
Senior Registered Mental Health Nurse

The sun was shining brightly as we sat on a wooden bench, enjoying every bit of warmth the sun had to offer. Sunlight glittered like gold as it hit the sea after almost a week of gloomy clouds. I was in my perfectly ironed blue uniform.

My patient looked at me for a moment and asked, "Do you miss the sun?"

I smiled and replied, "I am from India so yes, I miss the sun terribly."

She chuckled at the joy in my voice and asked, "Do you come from a city that has a shoreline?"

I turned to face her and said, "No, I come from a city that is landbound on all sides! One of the reasons I chose Portsmouth when I moved to the UK was because of the pretty pebbly beaches."

She looked at the sea and said, "The sea calms me. My mum used to take us to the beach every weekend. It's the most cherished memory that I have of my childhood."

We sat there and spoke for almost an hour, and then we had to return to the ward. We strolled back and reached my office.

The patient turned and spoke. "We should do this next week too; I feel a lot better."

I assured her that we could definitely do this again.

My fellow nurse stood near us, surprised – as he had just heard our patient speak for the first time in two weeks, since she had suffered a traumatic experience. Our patient had only been communicating her needs through written notes. The talking was a positive sign, a breakthrough that the whole team had been waiting for!

As I finished my shift and walked home, I was over the moon. I remembered the day I chose to become a mental health nurse. I chose to be a mental health nurse because I believed that there was healing to be done not only with medicine but also with kind words, the heart to listen and by just being there for your patient during their difficult times. And now I know that these simple things can bring great change in a patient's life.

If you think you have kindness in your eyes when you listen to others express their pain, and then can still stand by to guide them to get on with life, then please do not waste a single moment. Take courage and join the mental health nurse force because we need trailblazers like *you*.

More Than Meets the Eye

May Richell Parsons, *Modern Matron for Respiratory*

When I was nine years old, growing up in the Philippines, I loved helping my teacher with the younger kids during breaktime. It felt awesome to help, as well as play with the children, so when my mum asked me what I wanted to be when I grew up, I instantly said, "A teacher!" My mum reworded her question and asked: "But if you could be anything at all, what would it be?"

I thought about it, long and hard. I remember my mum having heart problems and my granddad having lung cancer. So, I said I wanted to be a doctor, so I could care for her and the rest of the family. But I had to have a science degree to go to medical school, so I chose nursing, thinking it would make me a better doctor if I also had the skills of a nurse!

It wasn't long before I got hooked on nursing. My first encounters with patients – seeing how important nurses are to their wellbeing – was enough for me to realize that this was what I wanted to do for my whole life.

There is so much more to nursing than meets the eye. During my training, I helped hundreds of mums give birth and also took care of their newborn babies. I looked after people with mental health issues, assisted surgeons in operations and went into local communities to give vaccinations. I promoted community health in poor areas, teaching patients about their conditions. I've guided nursing students on their own learning journeys – and I've done a lot more, as well, including being the first nurse in the UK to give a Covid vaccination!

There are so many different jobs within nursing, and out of everything, what I love most is the way I am helping everybody I meet. It makes me so happy and makes my heart full that my hands are there to care for people from when they are born until their last day. I treat all my patients as if they are my family and believe that everyone deserves the best of me and of our nursing services.

Nursing for me was my destiny, and is my calling and my passion. Covid has reaffirmed my belief that nurses are special human beings in so many ways and I'm eternally grateful for every one of them. I am so proud to be one, and hope that you might become one too!

No Two Days the Same

Kate O'Hagan, *Advanced Paediatric Nurse Practitioner*

I always knew I would be a nurse. My mum will tell you that she always knew, too. It was more my destiny than a career choice. I wanted to help and care for people. So, at the age of eighteen, I went to university and studied for a degree in 'children's nursing'. Then I went back to university at the age of twenty-five, and again when I was thirty! It's amazing how you can continue to learn every single day.

From Liverpool to London, then back again, I have had an exciting career where no two days have been the same. I have had the privilege of witnessing babies being born and of caring for children with an electric heart. I've transferred patients in helicopters, ambulances and even a plane.

During my time as a nurse, I have travelled to Honduras in Central America with a charity's team of doctors, surgeons and nurses. We performed heart surgery on children who were very ill, helping them to lead happier and healthier lives. I have travelled to Florida, USA to share my experiences in nursing and hear how nurses in different countries work, so that together we can improve our patients' care. I worked through the Covid pandemic, undertaking training on how to care for adult patients as well as children.

Your opportunities as a nurse are endless!

When you work as a nurse, you get to work with other nurses. Your work colleagues become your best friends and are like a second family. Nurses love to laugh, and we laugh a lot (and play tricks on each other, too!).

They say that if you choose a job you love, you will never work a day in your life – and I have never worked a day.

Precious Babies

Layla Lavallee, *Research Midwife*

Growing up in Canada, I was vaguely aware that midwives existed but knew very little about them. At that time, doctors looked after women while they were pregnant, nurses cared for them when they were about to have the baby, and doctors delivered the babies. Most people thought that was how it had to be done! In fact, it was illegal in Canada to have anyone but a doctor deliver a baby then.

My understanding of midwives changed when I moved to the UK in 1998. While working as a nurse in London (which I loved!) I met some student midwives. Hearing about their experiences, I instinctively knew it was what I wanted to do. I'd always been fascinated by pregnancy and childbirth and thought I'd eventually work in 'maternity nursing'. Had I grown up in the UK, where midwives are the norm, I'm certain I would have gone straight into midwifery training after finishing school.

In 2000, I enrolled on a midwifery degree programme. The first birth I attended was in the home of an incredibly chilled-out Dutch couple. I don't think I appreciated at the time how lucky I was to have such an easy introduction to childbirth, where everything went to plan by the couple's candlelight and a soundtrack of their favourite music!

Over the years, I have attended many more births, in all kinds of places. I've caught babies in cars, in baths, on floors, on yoga balls – and even in the hospital car park! One year a woman even gave birth under the Christmas tree in the hospital lobby.

No two births are ever the same but they're always precious, especially when the outcome is a sad one. Being a midwife sometimes involves loss and I remember every one of those mothers and babies I met whose stay in the world was far too brief.

I've worked with plenty of midwives throughout the years and they're a diverse bunch. My career has taken some unpredictable and exciting twists and turns, but I consider myself first and foremost a midwife, and feel very lucky to be one.

Why Choose Children's Nursing?

Karl Monaghan, *Matron Division of Medicine Complex Care Group*

"Why did you choose children's nursing?" This is a question I have been asked a *lot* throughout my life as a nurse. I have often wondered why I get asked this – is it because I'm male? Is it because it's believed that men are more likely to be doctors than nurses? Or because most male nurses work with adults and not children?

The reason I became a nurse was because of my own personal experience. When I was sixteen, I was injured in a camping fire on holiday. I had major burns to my legs, requiring lots of treatment and rehabilitation. Because of this, I met lots of different kinds of nurses. I wanted to become a nurse, too, so I could support and help people in difficult situations. I chose children's nursing because I always felt children were more vulnerable than adults and that being able to support children, as well as their families, was a challenge worth taking.

My nursing journey has taken me to many different places – there are so many exciting and important roles in the world of nursing.

I started my career on an orthopaedic ward, gaining lots of experience from broken limbs to children needing hip surgery. I then moved on to the intensive care department – it was like starting again as a newly qualified nurse! Then I moved to a children's accident and emergency department – another new experience, with new surroundings and new people. After a short time there, I joined the community nursing team and did some incredibly varied things, from carrying out home visits, working as a special needs school nurse, working with the palliative care team, and also working with the complex care service.

I am now a matron and draw on all of these experiences from the past twenty-odd years so I can continue to provide care and compassion to patients.

I have met so many amazing people over my career and met so many different challenges. Being part of improving services, supporting vulnerable families and working with teams that have huge hearts and a desire to care for people – *that* is why I chose children's nursing.

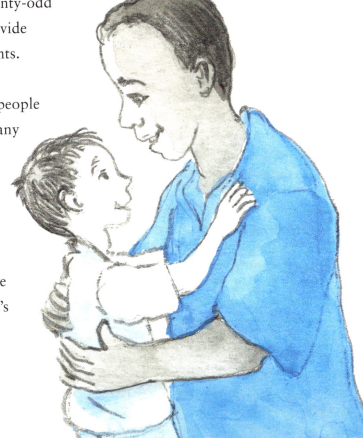

A Kind, Cheery Voice

Victoria White, *Clinical Nursing and Quality Manager*

I was always lucky to know growing up that I wanted to be a nurse. I remember friends calling me crazy – "How can you deal with blood and sick?!" I always had a fallback that if nursing failed me then I would become an air hostess as I could still look after people, but in the sky.

This motivation to become a nurse came from personal experience. As a young child I spent time in hospital and many days in my local doctor's surgery waiting to see my doctor or nurse, who by the time I was ten, knew me rather well. I remember sitting there one day hearing the phones ringing and the quiet chatting of patients sat in the waiting room – but the voice that stood out the loudest was the kind cheery voice of my local practice nurse. I remember saying I want that to be me one day.

In 2004, I started university on my chosen Adult Nursing course and those three years gave me the experience and skills to start my nursing career. My career took me to many places, working in hospitals and the community. I was able to meet a lot of interesting people from all walks of life and learn a lot. However, I always knew that nursing in a doctor's surgery was where I wanted to be. In 2016 I started my first nursing role in that same surgery I attended as a child. The same doctor who I had seen when I was younger was still there, though a little older and nearing retirement. I was then that nurse who started to see the children of friends I went to school with and the parents of those friends. I started to become the constant and recognizable friendly face, even when not at work.

Practice nursing gives the opportunity and privilege to support everyone when they are well, but also when people are at their sickest and in a moment of need. I have seen children grow and others pass on, but I get to know the families and understand their needs.

I have now moved on from my local surgery to expand my career in leadership in general practice and support new nurses and healthcare professionals, but the job remains the same – caring for the local population as a practice nurse, which I feel extremely honoured to be.

I am always grateful to those in my childhood who inspired me to become a nurse through their kindness and caring ways and I am always hopeful that I too can pass this passion on to the next generation.

Making a Difference

Jody-Ann Gordon, *Student Nurse, Children's Nursing*

"If you cannot figure out your purpose, figure out your passion, for your passion will lead you directly to your purpose" – T.D. Jakes

From a young age, I've been passionate about helping others. My main inspiration came from my grandmother, who nurtured me and was always willing to offer her care to others. As I grew up, I developed a genuine desire to care for vulnerable people, particularly children. My aim of becoming a children's nurse went beyond just 'helping others' – I had a deep desire to make a positive difference for poorly children and their families.

There are of course challenges in any career or area of life. As a student nurse, I have to balance and manage my time well, dealing with studies, work placements, part-time jobs and of course, my personal life.

Dealing with sad families can be difficult, but I understand how they feel, as I have felt scared and uncertain myself at times. I think that sharing my humanity with patients and their families is a gift.

I believe that my career path in nursing will be challenging in the future, but for the most part rewarding. It is indeed a beautiful thing when your career and passion come together. I strongly believe I have found my purpose through children's nursing!

Getting Joan to Drink More Water

Julia Terry, *Associate Professor*

I must tell you how I learned about 'doing with' not 'doing to'. What does that mean? Well, nurses always used to be known for doing things *to* people. Maybe this would be washing people, feeding people or taking people's temperatures. But now nurses know that patients get better faster if they do some things themselves.

This is a story about Joan. I met her when I worked in a hospital. I'm a mental health nurse and work with people who are often sad. Sometimes this means that people don't want to eat or drink and stop looking after themselves. The nurses on the ward told me that Joan wasn't drinking and was going to have a fluid chart, which meant everything she drank was written down on a list.

I knew it was important for the nurses to know how much Joan was drinking. The hospital team would ask about her daily drinking amounts

– they knew that if someone doesn't drink enough then they can have lots of problems. When people don't drink enough, they get dehydrated, often have wee infections, bad skin and find it hard to poo. So even if people don't feel like looking after themselves, they shouldn't want their health to get any worse, or they might end up with lots of other problems.

As nursing has changed over the years, there's been more reason to get people to take part in their own care. I thought that Joan might like to take part in keeping the fluid chart herself. I asked her, and she said she was interested in finding out more. So, we went into the kitchen together. I remembered that we had lots of different sizes of cups and beakers on the ward. So, Joan and I approached this as kind of project. Together we measured out how many millilitres was in a cup of tea and then how many in a beaker of water. This meant that every time Joan had a drink, she knew how many millilitres she had drunk. We wrote this on the chart.

Suddenly Joan was more interested because she was keeping her own records. We kept her fluid chart in the office because that's where the other notes were kept. And every time Joan had a drink or wanted a drink, she came to ask for her chart and filled it in. This sounds very simple but getting people to take part in getting better is really important. Doing things for people is not always the best way. Getting people to take part in their journey back to health means they become more independent.

This is still a new way for nurses to work. They used to think 'I'll do it, it's quicker'. But over time it's become much better to teach and show people how to be involved in their own care.

Nursing Children is a Joy!

Rohit Sagoo, *Children's Nurse*
and Director of British Sikh Nurses

"He's Punjabi? He's a children's nurse?!"

Being one of the first British-born Asian male children's nurses was a far cry from my mum and dad telling me to become a doctor, engineer or accountant!

After falling in love with the idea of working with children, I started my children's nursing career. I remember starting my first placement on a children's ward and seeing everyone run around like busy bees, and the high-pitched sounds of babies crying, drowning out the loud beep of machines in the background. For a second, I thought, how am I going to cope? Then a child lying on a bed spotted me. She saw my nerves and anxiety and called me over.

"You're a new student here, aren't you?"

"Yes!" I said.

And she began to tell me why she was in hospital and what her treatment was. I stood by her bedside in awe of this young lady – her resilience, strength and determination were just a marvel to see. That's when it hit me – I was definitely in the right place. This was where I belonged. This would be my career and was my calling, to care for children just like her.

Over the last twenty years I've cared for a lot of children, from those that came to hospital for a day, to those who stayed for a while, and to those who left for the heavens. Each child has a story, a personality and a smile. It's the smiles and laughter – especially the pranks they played on me! – that kept me going. But what I loved most of all was the care that we nurses delivered – we put every child at the heart of everything we do for them. We put them into our own hearts, too.

And now I teach new children's nurses. I find myself sharing my knowledge, experience and stories about my journey in children's nursing. To see student nurses develop, become confident and learn about the care needs of children is an amazing journey to witness and share.

Finally, I can say that my parents are proud of me! They hold their heads up high at Punjabi weddings and proudly say, "My son's a children's nurse!" After that I get bombarded by every auntie telling me their ailments, complaints and conditions. Thank goodness I only nurse children!

What can I say other than – nursing children is a joy!

The Good Times and the Bad

Lucy Bradford, *Advanced Clinical Practitioner for Older Persons' Care*

I have been in nursing now for over twenty-eight years. I always wanted to be a nurse. It was what I wrote down in primary school when we were asked what we wanted to be when we grew up. I remember drawing a picture of a girl in a uniform with a cap and a cape ... and writing that I wanted to be a nurse so I could look after people and make them better when they were ill. I followed my dream and look where I am now!

I remember the first day I put on my uniform – I was bursting with pride. The cap and the cape had sadly long gone, but nonetheless I looked smart and was so excited to get started!

Nursing has become my life. There is something so humbling about being privileged enough to be able to offer support to those less fortunate than myself. I have so many memories I could share, so many! But I will tell you of just one.

I was working in the intensive care unit, where the sickest patients are looked after in a hospital. We had a call to say a young man was coming in. He had had an accident on his motorbike and was very unwell. My consultant doctor asked me to get ready as we were going to try and do everything we could for this boy. He was nineteen years old.

When he arrived, we could see he was so sick. We worked very hard for hours and hours trying to support him until his body was strong enough to fight back. Day after day and night after night. I sat with his mum one night and she cried and told me she would never leave his side whatever happened. I thought about my own sons and knew that I would do the same.

After a month he left our unit to go to rehab. We didn't know what might happen to him as he was still not able to see or talk, so it was a bittersweet farewell for all of our staff, especially saying goodbye to his mum who had grown so attached to us all. Our nighttime chats kept her going, I'm sure.

A few months later I was at work, and I was asked to greet an old patient who wanted to see me again now he was on the mend. My heart skipped a beat when I saw the young man, standing up, walking, talking, even smiling! And his mum by his side with her eyes alight, thanking us for all we had done. Tears were shared that day!

That's why I do my job, through the good times and the bad. Even if the outcome is sometimes not what we are wishing for, we are in a position to make that time count. A nurse can make someone's last moments warm and safe or help a relative feel less scared or ease someone's pain by simply talking to them. What a privilege we have. I love my job.

A Full Heart

Asha Parmar, *General Practice Registered Nurse*

"Do come and be a nurse," they said. "You'll always have a job!"

I used to be a nurse in the accident and emergency department (A&E). I looked after the nans who had had a fall, I put up drips for the young people who were unwell. I saw kids with asthma and watched them get better with my care. I ran a lot and clocked up over ten thousand steps every day! I enjoyed that job. It was hard work, but I held hands and laughed with patients, and their families, too.

I now work in general practice (GP), you know, the doctor's surgery. I see the brand-new babies at only eight weeks old. I go to the homes of those who can't come out. I inject people to protect them against diseases. I dress wounds and cover up cuts. I fight for good health to help stop people from ending up in A&E. It's hard work, too, and challenges me, but it's a lot of fun being a part of the community in this way.

In both the GP surgery and A&E, we have regular visitors. I'd like to tell you about one of my regulars at the surgery. He is a man who had a troublesome wound on his foot for years. He didn't have much faith in modern medicine. I first saw him when I started to work at the surgery, but I don't think he liked me very much. But over the year that I saw him regularly, and we laughed a lot, he began to trust me more. For example, at first he said no to the Covid vaccine but when he found out that I was working at the clinic and could do his injection, he said yes. Fast forward to a year later, and he had a healed foot. He no longer had to cut his trainers for a comfortable walk. He didn't need to have a bandage on his foot every day. He came back one day and told me that it was my work that fixed him – but all I did was tell him how to look after his foot.

"Do come and be a nurse," they said. "You'll always have a job!" But they never told me that it wasn't only a job – they never told me that it would fill my heart for life.

Nursing Friendship

Jessica Davidson, *Clinical Nurse Lead for Justice*

M aureen was my first nursing friend when I was a newly qualified nurse. She was a health support worker and I was a beginner staff nurse on an orthopaedic ward.

Twenty-five years later, we are still close friends. We now live in different countries, but have helped each other through life's ups and downs. We went to dances together when we were young. I was her birth partner once; we went on wild Cornish walks; and we did *Thelma and Louise* trips where we would just point the car in one direction and drive!

Many of my close, most trusted friends are nurses, a range of ages, genders, backgrounds,

personalities and nationalities. We recognize each other. Although scattered all over the world, we recognize and understand each other.

What truly bonded us is: the trauma calls; nighttime emergency alarms; breaking bad news; mess and chaos; help and advice; training days; writing reference lists for essays; going to conferences; someone supporting your arm when you are stitching together a wound – upside down to reach a strange angle of a patient's body!

Nurses look out for each other and form the best of teams. We build protective walls around each other when tragedy strikes at home or work, often without any words needing to be said.

Oh, and we laugh, we laugh all the time! We laugh like mad, telling affectionate tales with humour. We laugh until the call of 'action' and then we are focussed professionals and exceptional communicators.

My nursing friends. I had no idea when I started training all those years ago that friendship was just as important to nursing as the knowledge and experience you gain. These friendships keep us going and help us to understand what it really means to be a nurse.

An Honour

Victoria Jackson, *Health Visitor*

I wanted to be a health visitor – a trained nurse who visits people in their homes – for so long, that I can't remember if I went into nursing to become a health visitor or if my very first placement when I was at university – which was with health visitors – inspired me to become one!

It wasn't a straight line from university to health visiting for me. I was able to experience many different parts of children's nursing, from looking after children following an operation or those with infections or mental health problems, to looking after babies born with heart and lung problems. I loved working with families whose children had heart and lung problems and I never ceased to be surprised when the day following open-heart surgery a child would be running all over the ward refusing to stay in bed, as if nothing had happened.

But health visiting continued to appeal to me and I became a qualified health visitor. It has been such an honour to visit families at home during the most wonderful time of their lives and also to help them in sadder times. Seeing a mother light up when her baby is finally breastfeeding well or the joy when a child finally sleeps through the night, or when you are thanked for listening to patients and helping them get the support they need.

The wonderful thing about being a health visitor is that it includes all parts of nursing and the family, so every day and every visit is different. But all visits have the same goal – to help prevent problems, for families to be happy and healthy and for children to be able to achieve their potential no matter if they have a disability or health problem.

I remember when I saw a pregnant mum with a toddler whose behaviour she was struggling with. The toddler was due his health review – this is when a health visitor checks on the mum and child to make sure they're doing okay – and the review showed that his speech was delayed. Between that visit and the final one, when the new baby was eight weeks old, I had helped the mum understand her child's behaviour and speech problems, both of which improved. She became happier and enjoyed spending time with her toddler and new baby – what could have been a sad and difficult time for the family became a happy and fun one.

And that is the best thing about nursing, whether it is in a hospital, community, school or online – helping someone to get better and seeing them smile, knowing that you have helped to change their life.

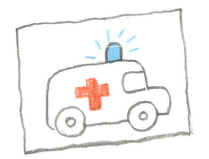

Nursing is a Noble Profession

Hephzibah Samuel, *Paediatric Nurse*

Nursing is a noble profession. Nurses are caring, compassionate people who know what to do when they look after you.

I am glad that I am a nurse – it is what I do best. It puts a smile on my face when I see children getting better. I know I have to do things that might be unpleasant, such as give medications and injections, but I only do this to make children feel better! They can even hold my hand tight when they are afraid or anxious.

It is a privilege to care for my patients. I go with children when they are taken to the operating theatre for surgery and look after them when they are back in the ward. I even make them warm toast with butter and jam when they are hungry. I am a good listener, and they can share their stories with me.

Nurses do many things to make hospital wards friendly places, such as decorating the walls with stickers and posters. Children can play with toys, read books, paint pictures and play games. There is often a playroom and an outside garden area. Some of my patients do baking and craft. They even make thank you cards for nurses and doctors!

One day, when a little girl was poorly, I had to give her a special medicine through a plastic tube in her hand. As I was giving it, I asked her what her favourite school subject was. She said science. Then I asked her what she wanted to become. When she said a nurse, I asked her why. She replied, "I want to be like you and help people."

As a nurse, I also take care of parents and carers because I know they are really worried about their poorly children. I answer their questions, tell them what's happening and explain any treatments.

Nursing is a noble profession. I hope that you might one day become a nurse too!

Life as a Nurse

Aisha Holloway, *Professor of Nursing Studies*

Thinking back to my childhood, I wasn't like everyone else at school. My mum is from Scotland and my dad is from Sudan in North Africa. The result was a baby (me!) born with warm golden brown skin and very curly hair.

At school I wanted to 'fit in', I guess. No one wants to be different, do they? But slowly my skin colour attracted the wrong kind of attention. I was called names, made fun of and I realized then what it was like to not quite 'fit in'.

There was no one in my family who was a nurse or had been a nurse. However, I used to watch my mum being so kind to everyone she met. She was always helping those who needed help or a friend.

My life and career as a nurse has been the most fulfilling, inspiring and privileged journey. It has been a place where I do fit in and it is where I belong. I am part of a family that stretches across the world. In every country, city and town, to the furthest corners, there is always a nurse.

My wish to become a nurse gave me a focus, gave me a purpose and an opportunity to be there for people in their hour of need – just as I had learned from my wonderful mum. So here I am, exactly thirty years later from graduating as a nurse, and I am a Professor of Nursing Studies. I have to pinch myself everyday and wonder, how did I make it here? I do a job that makes my heart sing.

My story is one of a young girl who was always herself, who knew the importance of feeling she belonged, who understood the joy of kindness, the pain of cruelty but was able to flourish and grow as a result of others' generosity. I was a young girl who wanted to change the world because of my own experiences.

My life as a nurse has been like no other. I have held the hands of those as they take their last breath. I have held in my arms the families of those who have died, offering comfort and sharing their grief. I have cried with happiness as those I have cared for have recovered and gone on to have fulfilling lives.

Today, my job means I get to teach young nursing students that the most important person they will ever lead is themselves. To walk in the direction of possibility and realize their potential. To see challenges as possibilities. To sit in the driving seat of their own lives. All of these are as important as the knowledge they will learn as part of their nursing education.

Today, my job means I get to work in collaboration with the world's greatest minds as we try to understand how we can meet the health challenges that the world faces. Together we undertake research to find the best ways to do this.

Today, my job means I work with nurse leaders, governments and global organizations to support the nurses of the future, to lift them up, to nurture them, to offer them opportunities and to show them the way to enable them to work to their full potential to ensure that care can be delivered to everyone everywhere.

Today, I am a nurse who still wants to change the world and I know I can … one step and each day at a time.

Ham and Cheese Toastie

Maritess Murdoch, *Quality Assurance Nurse, Care Homes*

It was the late 1990s when I decided to move to the UK from the Philippines to work as a nurse in a hospital. After a year, I applied for a job with a district nursing service in London. The district nursing service provides nursing care and treatment to people in their own homes.

I remember one morning, I left the office with a full list of patients to visit. It was going to be a busy day.

I first visited my patients who needed their medications and injections early in the morning. Then I set off to see one of my patients, Mary, who was in her late eighties and lived alone in a ground-floor flat.

Mary had a wound on her leg which needed to be checked and the bandages changed. As I opened the door, I heard her crying. She was upset. Her carer had been due to arrive at 9 a.m. to help her wash and dress but hadn't arrived yet.

I sat down next to her and said, "Why don't I make you a cup of tea and some breakfast?"

I saw her face light up as she said, "Would you?"

"Yes, of course!" I said. I asked her what she would like for breakfast.

Enthusiastically, Mary replied, "Ham and cheese toastie!"

"How do I make it?" I asked Mary. "Do you have a toastie maker?"

"No," she said, "just toast the bread, then spread the butter on the toast, then put on the ham, cheese, mayonnaise and mustard … in that order."

After her breakfast, I changed the bandage on Mary's wound. I put some food and water on her coffee table and made her another cup of tea. She said thank you and gave me the most beautiful smile.

As I left her flat, I took a deep breath and smiled. The sky was clear and the sun was starting to come out.

The smile never left my face. I felt a wonderful warm feeling in my heart. This was nursing. This was what nursing was all about.

Nursing was not just about assessing patients, giving medications, changing a bandage or checking blood pressure. It was about those small things that make a big difference to the lives of my patients.

Nursing was about compassion and generosity. I felt so happy that I made things better for Mary that morning. I walked towards the main road and shouted, "I love nursing!"

"Nursing? But I'm a Man!"

Suman Shrestha, *Consultant Nurse, Intensive Care*

Growing up as a teenager in Nepal was fun but I always felt something was missing from my life. I had an ambition to be someone and do something meaningful. I was desperately searching for an answer and for that opportunity.

I have an elder sister who has cerebral palsy. Ever since I was little, I had witnessed how she was cared for by my parents. It was instilled in me from an early age to be considerate, kind and caring towards people who are disabled and are vulnerable members of our society. My parents started a day centre for disabled children in place called Butwal in Nepal in 1994. This was one of the first in Nepal and brought massive awareness of learning disabilities locally and nationally. Today, the centre is much bigger and is attended by more than two hundred people with learning disabilities. I was actively involved in helping my parents with the day-to-day running of the centre, right from the beginning.

Nursing was never on my radar as a career option but after hearing about my involvement in the day centre, one of my dad's friends asked if I would be interested in coming over to the UK to study nursing.

"Nursing? Me? But I'm a man!" was my first response. Nursing back then (1997) was a female-dominated profession, and it still is now. I thought hard and decided to take on the offer as I felt that I had nothing to lose. If I didn't like it, I could always leave and do something else. How wrong was I?!

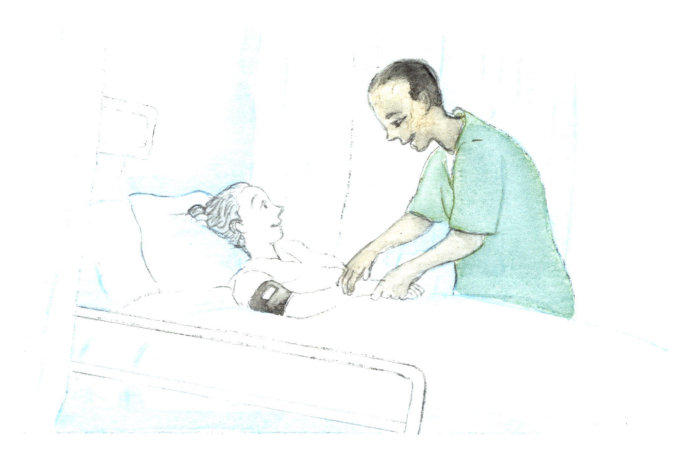

After completing my training, I started my nursing career working on different wards. I then went to intensive care as part of a programme for newly qualified nurses. This was when I realized where I wanted to work full time. Intensive care is where the most critically ill patients are looked after in hospitals. I was excited to learn about various diseases, physiology and medicine, and was really fascinated about the technologies and equipment used to support the life of those critically ill patients.

After studying some more and gaining lots of experience, I now work as a consultant nurse in intensive care. In this role I perform many of the skills usually done by doctors such as advanced physical assessment (where I check over how patients are), prescribing medicine, and so on. I also provide leadership to our team, and focus on education, training and research. I am a visiting lecturer at universities and have a national role representing intensive care nurses.

What I have learned over the last two decades is that nursing as a profession is dynamic and versatile with many opportunities.

I feel very privileged to do my job, looking after my patients, their families and friends during possibly the worst time of their lives in intensive care.

And by the way, you don't have to be of a certain gender to be passionate about caring for others!

Friends for Life

Dame Janet Elizabeth Murray Kershaw DBE FRCN,
Fellow of the Royal College of Nursing,
President, RCN 1994–1998

I t's been sixty years since I started training as a nurse, and much of what I was taught has passed into history due to the many innovations in care and treatment since.

But one thing has remained – the friendships made during those years. I have the membership list for the Retired Nurses Group from my training hospital, and I was recently reminded how strong those friendship ties are and how they supported us through not only our training days but since. I received a letter from one lifelong member:

"It is with a heavy heart that I write to tell you of the death of... We had been close friends since we started training in 1952."

I didn't know the writer personally although I expect I would recognize her if she was able to travel to our annual reunion. But her friend was

once my ward sister (in charge of my team), known throughout the hospital as being both capable and kind. I remember her with gratitude and acknowledge her skills in teaching me and the other students who crossed her path the ability to give compassionate care.

I fell then to thinking about my friendships from my training days. Two friends who live locally I see regularly; a third I am in touch with through email and telephone whilst others I see only from time to time.

Those same friends who all those years ago helped me through training – the weariness of a hard shift, the death of a patient known for some time, the poor mark from a piece of written work or the dismay of being allocated to a placement where the ward sister was known to be 'difficult'. Those friends have been there for ever. They were present at my wedding, at the premature birth of my son, the death of my brother and most recently we helped each other through the isolation of Covid.

Nursing has not only given me friends from all those years ago. Through the Royal College of Nursing (RCN), I have friends all over the world. Some I hope to see again at national and international nursing conferences, while others I meet from time to time online.

Nursing – and I am sure midwifery is the same – gives you so much more than learning to care. It offers friends for life.

A Prison Nurse

Simon Newman, *Head of Prison Health and Wellbeing*

As a teenage boy I suffered a knee injury playing football which led me to being hospitalized and having an operation. I had many visits over time to my local hospital during which I observed the staff working, and alongside the hard work I could see going on, I could also the fun that they were having.

As I went through high school, I chose subjects that might help me towards a career in nursing but perhaps didn't share this ambition with others as I was conscious that this would be an unusual choice for a boy in the 1980s.

I spoke to a relative who was a nurse and explored the different types of nursing careers I might pursue. I had an interest in the military and also emergency care, these being options that might give me the opportunity to travel and live in different places.

What I didn't expect, eight years into what is currently my thirty-six-year career as a nurse, was to arrive on a Monday in a new nursing role in a prison and spend my first day being given a bunch of keys on a chain attached to a belt around my waist, be taught how to open cell doors and be immersed in a noisy prison environment.

I have now been a nurse in prisons for over twenty years. It is completely different to being a nurse in almost all other places.

The variety of work you undertake is huge and the patients range from teenagers to the elderly. We work hard, but similarly to the nurses I saw as a teenager, we do have a lot of fun.

Although I haven't had the career I expected to have, I have always enjoyed working as a nurse in prisons. I chuckle at people's responses to my saying I'm a nurse, "What, a male nurse?" And when I say I work in prisons, "What, you're a nurse in a prison?!"

I Didn't Always
Want to Be a Nurse!

Natalie Pattison, *Professor of Nursing Critical Care*

Funnily enough, I didn't always want to be a nurse, unlike some of my friends who knew since they were little that was what they wanted to do. In fact, I was going to study something completely different, but I'd chosen to take a gap year between school and university and found myself volunteering in a Red Cross hospital on the other side of the world. It opened my eyes to working with patients, and I realized how much difference nurses could make to the experiences of patients and families. I went to university to study nursing, and when I'd finished my training, I started working in cancer care. I then moved into working in critical care (also called 'intensive care'), the part of the hospital that cares for the sickest patients.

I loved learning about why things happened and understanding what we needed to do to make things better. I saw that research was really important. Health research is about fact-finding and problem-solving in

an organized way and helps us decide how to treat people. It was clear there were some areas that nurses, doctors and the healthcare team knew very little about. Working in critical care, I was looking after people who often could not talk or care for themselves.

I am lucky enough to work leading research in this area and apply what our research tells us to the care of patients and families. I now look after patients who have come out of critical care to help them in their recovery.

One of the things that has stayed with me is when we admitted a pregnant woman called Lucy and she became very poorly. We were all really worried when she was in critical care. Afterwards, she had a lot of health problems, but I was able to help her with those. When she finally gave birth a few weeks later, I was able to go and see her and meet her healthy, beautiful baby boy. It was such a happy, joyous occasion. A few months later, she even brought him to the critical care unit so the team could meet him and see how they'd saved her life and his life. It was very emotional and wonderful to see how our work can make things better for the sickest people.

The Smiley Nurse

Nichole McIntosh, *Regional Head of Nursing and Midwifery*

I remember when I first became a nurse and worked in the East End of London. I enjoyed the experience of caring for patients who had many different needs. I was a young Jamaican-born nurse and had recently migrated to England. I approached my work in a relaxed and caring way to ensure that all around me felt calm. I remember that I was so happy to be a nurse that I smiled a lot. Eventually, I became known as the 'smiley nurse'. I even heard some patients whispering that 'the smiley is here' when I arrived for work one day. My heart smiled that day and I still smile every time I think of it.

I had always wanted to be a nurse so when the chance came to train, I grabbed it with both hands. I have never regretted it, it is the best decision I have ever made. I could not see myself doing anything else. Caring for others comes naturally to me and I get a deep sense of satisfaction to think that I am helping others to get better.

I would like to encourage others to consider nursing as a career to get a taste of what I have experienced. This is what what the letters in the word 'nurse' mean to me:

N U R S E

N is for the **nurturing** and healing power that nurses effortlessly display;

U is for the **unrivalled** compassion that every nurse shows that brings peace to patients, night and day;

R is for the **resilience** that no other professional can match;

S is for the **servitude** that nurses freely provide;

E is for the **empathy** for our patients, their families, our colleagues, always given with a smile.

I hope to inspire the next generation of nurses to carry on caring for patients with kindness, compassion and a smile.

I Would Do It All Again

Janette Streeting, *Diabetes Specialist Nurse*

As I approach my retirement, I can't help but remember about some of the experiences I have had during my career. I have met some wonderful and inspiring people and have touched the lives of so many others.

My career in nursing began when my parents dropped me off in a small room with a sink, wardrobe, bed and a desk at the tender age of nineteen, which would become my home for the next few years. I often think back to my interview to be accepted into the NHS family and was asked questions such as, "Why do you want to become a nurse?" I think my answers may be different now if asked again!

I have seen many changes over the past forty years. Nursing has moved on and nurses are not only giving patients their medicines but prescribing them too. The role has changed, and nurses are more respected by the medical profession now.

49

As student nurses back then, you didn't speak to the ward sister unless you were spoken to and certainly not the consultant (a doctor who specializes in one area of medicine). They were scary people! Nurses were expected to keep busy and if you didn't have anything to do you went and found something. There was always a bed pan that needed scrubbing!

Life as a nurse is very different now and the role is much more respected with nurses taking on advanced skills and specialist roles. The doctors now come to us for advice. Oh, how times have changed! But I have had a great career and wouldn't change a thing. I would do it all again.

A Great Service

Claire Roche, *Executive Director of Nursing and Midwifery*

For most of my career, I worked in midwifery. I had lots of different jobs and roles as a midwife. I worked in the community providing care and support for mums and babies, as well as working in busy hospital maternity units where mothers give birth and care for their new babies.

In 2014, I had a job in Wales where I set up the first Maternity Network. The network helped midwives, doctors and anyone who worked in maternity services or who used them to share ideas and improve maternity care. This was a really exciting and interesting time as I had to learn new skills and travel all over the country meeting lots of new people and hearing about different and new ways of working.

This led me to a new and exciting job with an ambulance service. I first worked at the Welsh Ambulance Service as an Assistant Director

for Quality Governance. Quality governance is about monitoring how well we do things and understanding where we need to improve. This is important as learning how we can improve services for the people who use them means that we can better meet peoples needs, and ensure they are safe and have a good experience.

After working at the ambulance service for three years, I then got the post of Executive Director of Quality and Nursing. Being an 'executive' means you have a voice at the Trust Board. The Trust Board is a group of people responsible for the service and how it runs.

Today, I have a new job, I am the Executive Director of Nursing and Midwifery at Powys Health Board in Wales. All of my experiences to date have really helped me to be able to do a job like this. I am very proud to be the nursing and midwifery representative at the Board and to be able to lead nurses and midwives so that we can provide a great service.

A Proud Nurse

Cecilia Anim, *Clinical Nurse Specialist,*
President RCN 2015–2018

I was born in Sekondi, Ghana and lived near a maternity home. I remember declaring, at age two, that I wanted to be a 'bigwife' and it was in that moment that my journey to where I am today began.

At the age of twenty-one, I qualified as a midwife and went to work in a village health centre in Ghana. This was an eye-opening and rewarding experience as I was the only midwife carrying out nursing duties for a large population, with a doctor visiting only weekly.

I decided to come to England to further my nursing education. There I qualified as a nurse – and was also introduced to the delights of fish and chips and a proper cup of tea! But despite the excitement of being somewhere new and different, I still had moments of homesickness.

I moved to London and had a few different nursing roles. They opened my eyes to inequality within the workplace, so I joined the Royal College of Nursing (RCN) for support and to campaign against inequality. I have learnt along the way the importance of working in collaboration with others to create a lasting change for both patients and nurses.

In 2009, I became deputy president of the RCN. I changed from being an activist to a leader, from being angry into being engaged. In 2017, I was awarded a CBE by the Queen for services to nursing.

My nursing journey has taken me to different countries and I've met the great and the good. I remain eternally grateful for all the opportunities I've had to care for patients, especially those roles where we had to learn to turn scarcity and limitations into an advantage. It taught me resilience, humility and compassion. These are the skills that I draw on every day in my nursing career.

Throughout it all, I have never forgotten the two-year-old me from Sekondi who wanted to be a 'bigwife'. My roots and my heritage are a part of me and I have no desire or need to hide that or pretend to be something other than what I am: a proud nurse and a proud Ghanaian.

Chase Your Dreams

Linsu Boniface, *Learning Disability Health Facilitator*

Waking up every day to bright sunshine with the chirping of sparrows and robins was delightful for me when I lived in India. However, working as nurse in India did not help me to pay the cost of rent, food and bills, or help me pay for the cost of further education so I could pursue my dream of becoming an advanced nurse practitioner. How can a wage of less than £200 a month make all the ends meet?

Even though the pay was low, it was so satisfying to work as a nurse, to help the needy, heal the ill. I slept peacefully every night by thinking of the people I helped, the wounds I dressed, the tears of the ill patients and their relatives that I wiped. But I hoped there would be light waiting for me at the end of the tunnel so I could chase my dream of training as an advanced nurse practitioner.

One day, the magic fairy waved her wand on me and carried me to

England to work as a nurse in an NHS hospital. I worked in the hospital as an intensive care nurse for nearly three years, but my dream of being a nurse practitioner did not die.

One day I remembered what my dad had once said: "Come out of your comfort zone to chase your dreams and fly high in victory!"

So I took his advice and that's when the real magic happened in life. I jumped to a higher-up nursing role. I achieved this all by myself, powered by my lifelong dream, and I stand now with my head held high, with joy and dignity.

If you have a dream of nursing like I did, please don't be afraid to chase it!

Nursing Teaches You So Much

Professor Alex McMahon, *Scotland's Chief Nursing Officer*

hen I was a young boy, I never thought of becoming a nurse. Most of the nurses I knew or saw were women, so I didn't think of it as a career for men. I was wrong!

I knew what I wanted to do: work hard at school, go to art college and study graphic design. I wanted to illustrate books and album covers as I was really into art and being creative. But one day a teacher said to me, "Alex, I think you would make a really good nurse!" She thought of me as someone who cared for others, in that I looked out for my friends and would say something if I thought that they hadn't been treated fairly.

I liked this teacher a lot, and after thinking it through I applied for a nursing course in my local area. Now I've got her to thank because she was right – nursing was my calling!

I started my nursing career in 1983 and have just never stopped! I qualified as both a mental health nurse and a general nurse. Although hard work at times, my nursing career has been full of great experiences. I have loved all the different skills I've mastered and the ways I've learned to help people get well. When my patients couldn't get better, I've supported them and their families in the best way I could. Nursing teaches you so much and opens you up to skills that you can use throughout your life.

Today, I lead the nursing profession in Scotland. That's a huge responsibility! All my years as a nurse have given me the experience to do this job and be able to make a positive difference to all of Scotland's nurses. It's a role based in the Scottish government where I can help develop nursing so that it continues to be the best job in the world, so that the nurses of today and tomorrow can deliver high-quality health services in the future.

If you haven't thought about being a nurse, please do! I would especially encourage boys and young men to think about it as only nine per cent of the whole nursing workforce are men – but it should be a job for everyone. Trust me when I say that you will thrive on the challenges of nursing, from working with older people and children, to working with people with learning disabilities or those needing help with their mental health. There's a nursing role out there for everyone.

You never know – one day you could be a chief nursing officer for Scotland, too!

The Missing Leech

Jacqui Tahari, *Research Nurse*

Whilst working on the plastic surgery ward, sometimes we were asked to use leeches to aid with the recovery of a finger or toe that had been in an accident – and that the surgeons had had to sew back on! Well, I don't like leeches, but I had to do this as it was my job!

The leeches were put on to the tip of the finger or toe to suck out the blood. When the leech was full (you could see this as they got very fat!) the nurse would take the leech away. One time, when I was working nights and it was dark, I had to remove a leech from a child's toe. I took a piece of gauze and with gritted teeth I picked up the leech, put it into a bowl with the gauze (so I couldn't see it!) and walked down the ward to the sluice room, where waste is disposed of. But when I opened the gauze, the leech wasn't there! Imagine my horror as I thought it may have dropped on to me! I think I might have screamed a little, and I shook my uniform – luckily it wasn't there.

I calmed down and thought I may have dropped the leech on the ward, so I retraced my steps, using a torch to look all around. But I still couldn't find it! I went into the cubical where the child was, and the mum was standing there too. Then, just by the mum's foot, I spotted ... the big fat leech! I said quietly to the mum, "Don't move!" – I had an image of her standing on it and it squirting everywhere!

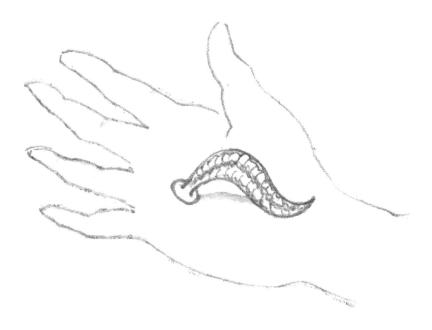

I managed to pick it up and dispose of it safely.

What a relief!

The Nurse Who Held Their Hand

Jessica Anne Filoteo, *Staff Nurse*
(Cardiac Catheterisation Laboratory)

I work in a department where we treat people who need minor heart operations. We help patients who have had heart attacks among other things. It's a huge, very busy, very fast-paced department.

One day I had a patient coming in to have his pacemaker battery changed. A pacemaker is a device that is placed inside someone's body to help their heart beat in the right way. This procedure involves having medicine to numb the area before the skin is cut, the old battery removed and replaced with a new one, and the skin stitched up again. We also give patients some medicine through their veins to help ease the pain and make them more comfortable.

We tend to be more cautious with older patients because they are often more sensitive to such medications and unfortunately for this patient, that was the case. He was quite nervous during the procedure, so after

I had given him small doses of medicine to calm him down, I sat beside him, held his hand and offered him reassurance until the procedure was finished.

Before he left the room, he grabbed my hand, looked me in the eye and said, "Thank you for holding my hand, that really meant a lot to me."

A few months later, this same patient wrote a letter to express his gratitude. In his letter he said, "At one stage the nurse offered to hold my hand and that kind act made the world of difference. Eventually the operation was completed, and I thanked the surgeon and his staff and also told the nurse she had given me much comfort."

Too often, big busy departments put a lot of pressure on nurses, and we get caught up in just trying to get things done. We forget the personal side of the care we provide to patients. I always try to pause every time I encounter a new patient. I remind myself that this is someone's son, someone's dad or grandpa. Somewhere out there, they have a family anxiously waiting for news that their procedure went well, and they're going to be okay.

I always ask myself, if this was my own parent, how would I want their nurse to look after them? This shift in thinking is what keeps me going especially on challenging days. It's my own little reminder that I have this privilege, that not many people have, to make a difference in someone's life. My patients may not remember my name, but to them I will always be that nurse who held their hand.

The Best Bits of Nursing

Nicola Ring, *Professor of Nursing*

When I was seventeen, I left home to begin my life as a student nurse. Looking back, I only had a vague idea what being a nurse meant – that I would work in a hospital and wear a uniform. Having been a qualified nurse for a very long time, I can say now that whilst many nurses do work in hospitals and wear uniforms – nursing and being a nurse is way more than that!

Everyone knows that the best bit about being a nurse is the people you work with – patients, their families and your colleagues. But not everyone knows that another best bit is the opportunity available to you as a nurse – the opportunities are huge! Over my career I have worked in hospitals and in people's homes; in uniform and in my own clothes; on shifts/rotas and on regular Monday to Friday 9 to 5 hours. I have worked in the UK and I have been lucky enough to have worked abroad. That is one of the great things about nursing – there is something for everyone!

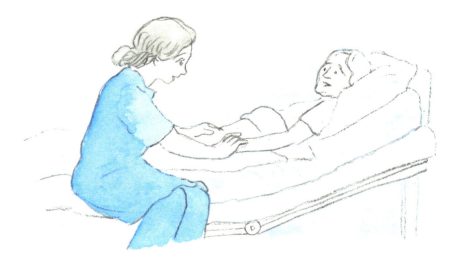

Over my career I have been fortunate to have had some fabulous mentors and role models – one was a health visitor who also worked in a university. Seeing her work with families and then hear about her teaching and research made me want to become a nurse lecturer. So I went to work in a university teaching nursing students. I love it! I love working with the new first-year students and watching them grow into qualified nurses. I love working with qualified nurses who want to develop their careers by undertaking further study and learning to do their own research.

A few years ago, someone in my family was seriously ill and during that time, I came into contact with lots of nurses who had been my students. Whilst this was an awful time for my relative and my family, the fabulous nursing care made everything so much better. That's when I realized there was another best bit about nursing – helping to develop the next generation of nurses and seeing them work so well in support of their patients and families. Maybe after reading the stories in this book, I will have the privilege of teaching you one day, too!

A Huge Privilege

Hannah Grace Deller, *Paediatric Matron*

In March 2020, I realized that Covid was here, and most likely here to stay. When I say stay, I thought it would be for a few months. I can remember reassuring friends, telling them that it would be over pretty soon. The rumblings at work had begun, and we were told that we needed to support our adult colleagues, as the admissions for children at this time were unusually low. We changed our children's ward and intensive care unit (ICU) to adult Covid units, and my journey of looking after adult patients began.

We were the only children's department that I know of in the UK that changed to be an adult ward with a team of children's nurses caring for the sick. It was a huge privilege to be asked to help, and even though I wasn't trained to nurse adults, I jumped at the chance to make a difference in these unusal times.

Patients started to be admitted to the ward, one after another, a lot of whom were, sadly, very poorly. I'd never experienced this level of sickness and loss before and at times it was completely overwhelming. As I was now the matron – in charge of the new adult ward but also the children's ward – I felt a huge sense of responsibility for not just the patients and their families, but for staff, especially the junior members of the team. Most of the time I kept my emotions and fears to myself and processed my feelings through my other creative outlet – photography.

Creativity throughout the pandemic was like therapy for me. I can remember the first photograph I took at work of a colleague in ICU. It was one of the domestic cleaners and he was stuck in the one-way system trying to get out of the door, laden with rubbish bags from his department. I saw his face in the window looking lost and bewildered and he reminded me of a character from a movie I'd seen about a nuclear explosion.

As well as snatching these experiences on camera I would jot down thoughts and feelings in a notepad. It helped me process my feelings and the profound experience I was having.

I've always felt it was a huge privilege to be involved in saving lives – most people don't get to experience it in their lifetime let alone on a daily basis. I found that even in the darkest times there were extraordinary emotions at work – in the holding of a hand in someone's last moments, in the intimacy you share with your patients when you're nursing them, and that special moment you celebrate when your patient is discharged and sent home. Life is precious and through nursing I have come to see our shared humanity. What more could you ask for in life than to be connected to people in this way?

Overcoming a Fear

Carlito Adan, *Senior Research Nurse*

My family is a one of teachers, engineers and businesspeople. No one has ventured in the field of medicine or healthcare – until me!

When I was young, I always fainted at the sight of blood even if it was just a droplet. That is why everyone was surprised, when one day, I went home from college and I told my parents that I would be shifting from an accountancy course to a nursing course! Of course, their jaws dropped and I could see disappointment on their faces, questions started flying to my direction – "Are you sure?", "What are you going to do when you see blood?", "What are you thinking?", "Maybe you are just confused!", "Give yourself some time to think about it."

At that young age of fifteen, when I started going to college, I stayed true to myself and I followed my heart to study nursing. I enjoyed my time as a student nurse – learning about human anatomy, clinical procedures and most importantly the caring aspect of the profession. Did I faint when I saw blood? Yes, I did on several occasions but it got better throughout my journey. The fainting became just feeling dizzy, until one day I realized that I had completely overcome my fear.

The next thing I knew, I was hopping on a plane from the Philippines to become a nurse in the United Kingdom!

Being a nurse has made me more compassionate and resilient. It is a very fulfilling profession, especially when you see people under your care get better – from grimaces to smiles, sorrows to hope, and sadness to joy! Challenges? There are many! Regardless of your profession, challenges are part of it. They are there to teach us life lessons and they make us better at what we do.

As a profession, nursing is very diverse; there are so many specialities to choose from, such as caring for children or the elderly, or working in cardiac (hearts) or neurology (brains!) – the list goes on.

In my case, being a nurse has offered me many opportunities, and I am now a research nurse. It is very rewarding to be a part of a team that informs, innovates and helps make a difference and improve patient outcomes. And for that, I have never regretted choosing to be a nurse!

"My Nurse, Maggie"

Margaret Bayley, *Retired Chief Nurse*

When I was about five years old, I got my first nurses' uniform and used to dress up in it all the time! Both of my aunties were nurses, and my mum worked as a district nurse, so I think nursing just came naturally to me.

I want to share two stories that happened during my forty-year career as a nurse, to show you just how special the people I looked after were.

When I was working in London, I met a lovely couple called Renee and Jack, both about eighty years old. Jack was very poorly and wanted to go on holiday again with Renee for what would probably be the last time. Imagine my shock when Jack's doctor volunteered my services to be their travel assistant and nurse!

So, off I went to Hayling Island for five days with Jack and Renee. It was such a memorable part of my career to be able to share Renee and Jack's last holiday together. They will always be a part of my life; in my memories and in my heart.

The second story is from my time working with children. I thought this was a bit scary, really, as I was used to looking after adults, not children! So, I popped across to Great Ormond Street Hospital and did some training with them to make sure I knew what I was doing.

I looked after a very special boy, who was very poorly. I went along to his school assembly and met all of his classmates and the whole school. We went up on to the stage to explain everything about his care. He introduced me as, "My nurse, Maggie." I was both humbled to be 'his' nurse and proud by his acceptance of his illness. I'll never forget the experience, or the special little boy.

I can honestly say that I have valued and loved every single day of my career, and all those special people that I've been allowed to look after. You can never do too much for people; sharing and being part of their lives when they are at their most vulnerable, during both happy and sad times, is absolutely inspirational.

Being a Research Nurse Rocks!

Femke Steffensen, *Clinical/Research Nurse Specialist for Difficult Asthma*

I am a research nurse!

Sounds boring at first, doesn't it?

Sounds like reading all day long, writing essays and not really seeing any patients.

But I tell you, being a research nurse is amazing!

I help to invent new treatments and drugs for patients with many different and rare diseases, such as new cancer treatments or new drugs for poorly children.

Recently, I helped to make a Covid vaccine. I phoned patients to ask if they'd like to take part in testing it, then I helped the doctor in assessing whether the patient could have the vaccine or not. I also prepared the vaccine and gave it to patients as an injection.

After giving the injection to patients, they came back to see me so I could check they were feeling well and healthy. After these checks and after the government was happy the new vaccine was safe, people all over the United Kingdom were allowed to have it.

You see, being a research nurse rocks!

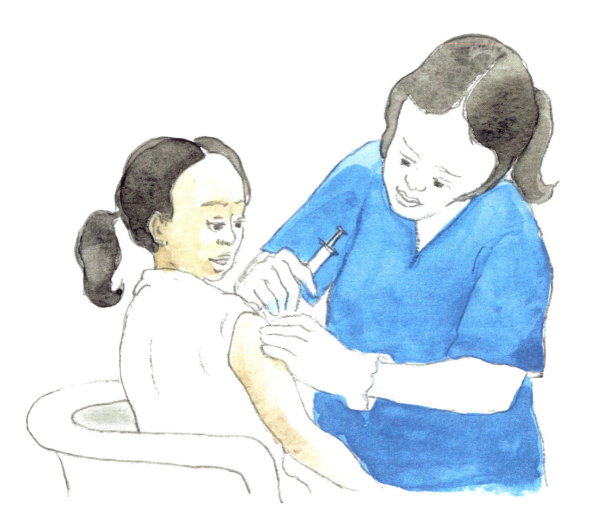

Nurses are the Backbone

Robert Sowney, *Independent Healthcare Consultant*

From a very young age I always knew I wanted to be a nurse. My family and friends thought I was confusing my choice with wanting to be a doctor, as nursing was not such a popular choice for men years ago; however, I was very clear it was a nurse that I wanted to be.

I understood the role of a nurse as being different to that of a doctor, how nurses were the backbone of the hospital or community setting, how nurses were the constant, the builders of relationships, the compassionate individuals with emotional intelligence and empathy. They had the ability to care physically and emotionally at the same time.

My proudest moment in life was when I achieved that dream, the day I could call myself a nurse. It was also a very proud moment for my parents as there were no other nurses in the family.

I only ever wanted to be with patients at the bedside – caring, supporting and helping others in their time of need. I have travelled to many parts of the world because of being a nurse, and I have worked in many different roles within nursing from bedside nursing to leading large groups of not only nurses but other professionals as a senior nurse within a hospital. I have also worked in and managed an ambulance service. These roles can be just as rewarding because you are supporting others to achieve and be the best they can be, to the benefit of patients and those in need.

I believe nursing has prepared me to be a very diverse person. It has taught me many skills which can be applied to lots of other roles. There are not many professions which give you the ability and skills to do anything you want to, that give you the confidence to take on challenges that you never thought you could or seize opportunities that you never thought you should.

The camaraderie within nursing – the colleagues that have become true and best friends, the feeling of being part of a wider family or community – is not something that everyone experiences in their chosen career, and it is something that I treasure and am very grateful for.

Nursing is not for everyone and there are times, like everything else in life, when we may question our choices. However, if I had to do it all again I absolutely would. There is no greater privilege than supporting and helping children and their families at the beginning of life, continuing to provide that care and support as they face illness throughout their life, and of course the greatest privilege of all, providing care and support at the end of life.

An Exciting Adventure

Jade Stewart, *Specialist Community Public Health Nurse*

I n 2015, I took a brave and exciting step to leave my home in the countryside and move to London to train as a public health nurse (a nurse or midwife who specializes in an area such as promoting a healthy lifestyle).

After a year of living in London, I found out about a new project working with one of the leading health organizations in England, who were looking to recruit qualified nurses to become 'clinical nurse champions for physical activity'. I was offered the role, which was a few hours a month, and could be carried out alongside my current job. I was over the moon!

I set off on a mission to help spread the word about the benefits of physical activity and approached lots of different groups of nurses to ask if they would allow me to visit them. Most nurses were student nurses, mental

health nurses and practice nurses who worked at doctor's surgeries. The nurses invited me to their training days and lunchtime learning meetings and it was my job to share the latest research with them and encourage them to talk to their patients more about becoming more active.

They say you should practise what you preach and there is nowhere better than London to try out some new activities. I tried everything, from yoga in a skyscraper, swimming in an outdoor lido and even water sports on the River Thames (accidentally falling in the Thames in November without a wetsuit on is not advised – so please try not to follow my lead on that one!). Nursing can open up so many amazing life opportunities!

Proud to Be Called a Nurse

Francesca Steyn, *Fertility Nurse Specialist*

When I was growing up, my nan always used to tell me that I would make a great nurse. After I left school and had started my nurse training, I'd completely fallen in love with it and knew that my nan was right. I qualified as a general nurse for adults when I was twenty-one and found my way into women's health and fertility. I've now been a fertility nurse specialist for seventeen years. In this role I help women who are pregnant or hoping to have babies.

I have been extremely lucky to have had a very exciting career and it still fascinates me every day to be involved in human reproduction and to see how microscopic egg and sperm cells come together to create life.

During my time as a nurse, I have been able to present my work and share my experiences both nationally and internationally. I've travelled to Uganda to speak about fertility nursing to a group of African fertility nurses and I led the first ever nursing event at the International Federation of Fertility Societies World Congress in Shanghai, China.

Although there have been very many happy times in my role, there has also been a lot of sadness as unfortunately not every person who tries to have a baby will succeed, so there can be a lot of heartbreak. But knowing that I was able to support my patients through those hard times has been extremely rewarding.

There is a quote from the poet Maya Angelou that I always share when I speak about nursing as it's so important to make people feel supported and safe: "I've learned that people will forget what you said, people will forget what you did, but people will never forget how you made them feel."

Nursing isn't for everyone, but I can honestly say that I would never want to do anything else. I have loved every moment and am extremely proud to call myself a nurse.

The Nurses
and the Donkey

Laura Jayne Simms, *Registered General Nurse*

Have you ever met a nurse? If so, you may know lots of powerful stories about how amazing they are.

I'm going to tell you a story about nurses. Nurses AND a donkey. As you read or listen to this, you may want to think about the qualities of the nurses in the tale.

In this story, the nursing team all worked at a hospice. A hospice is where people who are living with illnesses or conditions that can't be made completely better can go to stay. Hospices often have 'specialist' nurses and other staff that visit people at home. They also have senior nurses that help run the hospice itself, nurses that lead clinics and drop-in centres, and some hospices have bedrooms and nurses where people come to stay when they need extra help and support for a while. The hospice in this tale did just that.

One day the nurses had a meeting. A woman (let's call her June) had come into the hospice to get some help and was feeling very poorly. June had always loved animals and was the owner of lots of donkeys! Some people have goldfish or dogs, but June had donkeys. She was really missing her favourite donkey, and the donkey was missing June. So, the nurses had an idea, and hatched a plan with June's family. Can you guess what the idea was?

The day of the plan arrived. The sun was shining, and the nurses were ready. One had checked that the donkey was allowed to come to the hopsice; another had spoken to all the staff and patients to prepare them. Another had helped June have a jacuzzi bath and adjusted her medicine so that she was feeling tiptop.

Yes, you guessed it – the donkey came to visit! The family arrived with the donkey van and, cautiously, the little grey-brown donkey was led out, enticed by a carrot. He was led around the side of the building to June's bedroom where she was resting, and SURPRISE! June's favourite donkey was right there, braying loudly, excited to see and smell his lovely human. They cuddled and nuzzled, and June cried with happiness. Some of the nurses cried too. Some with glad hearts and one because the donkey did a big poo in the corridor.

The nurses in this team all had different jobs, but worked together using

their skills, expertise and compassion, to find out what mattered most to June, and made it happen for her. June sadly died that same year, as was expected with her illness, but she and her family were able to share lovely memories and photos of that amazing day.

I hope that you liked this donkey story. It might have made you think about the extraordinary difference that nurses and healthcare staff make to people's lives.

It may even have inspired you to think about becoming a nurse yourself. I do hope so.

Determined to Be a Nurse

Karen Jephson, *Community Neurological Rehabilitation Nurse*

When I was a little girl, I always wanted to be a nurse. I don't really know why – I didn't have any relatives that were nurses. I was very disappointed and upset at the end of senior school when I was told by the career advisor that I 'wasn't clever enough to be a nurse'.

I only left school with one GCSE equivalent – so I went to sixth form and got six more! I was determined to be a nurse. I was offered a place at nursing school (it wasn't university in those days). I moved from the Midlands to the sunny south coast when I was eighteen to begin my nurse training.

In 2023, it will be forty years since I was that eighteen-year-old! Over those years I have worked in lots of different nursing roles. I've worked on wards and in intensive care. For many years I worked in hospice care, looking after patients with life-limiting illnesses. I also worked in the first

89

HIV/AIDS hospice in the UK in the 1990s – when lots of people were ill and died because of AIDS.

I then returned to studying (university this time) and qualified as a district nurse. So, for twenty-seven years I have worked as a community nurse, realizing this is where my heart lay. To begin with I worked as 'general'/community nurse – looking after patients in their own homes. Visits could be for an injection, to dress a wound or look after someone who was very ill. Then I chose to 'specialize' – so for the last thirteen years I have worked in the community helping people to recover from neurological, or brain, injuries. I now work alongside other professionals all doing our own bit to make up the whole care of any one patient. Brain injury includes stroke, which can affect almost every aspect of someone's life from their mobility to their memory and can be life-changing.

Part of my role is helping patients to look after themselves – to reduce their risks of another stroke happening. Sometimes it's helping patients to look after their blood pressure or to make positive lifestyle changes or just to understand what's actually happened to them. A neurological 'event' can be very frightening.

Over the past almost forty years I've been involved in some incredibly sad and humbling stories, and some amazing ones too – many I will never forget. I've worked alongside dedicated nurses and healthcare professionals who work tirelessly for patients and their families.

It's a shame I never got to let that careers advisor know that I actually did okay as a nurse!

Dreaming of Florence Nightingale

Dame Anne Marie Rafferty, *Professor of Health and Nursing Policy, Florence Nightingale Faculty of Nursing, Midwifery and Palliative Care*

When I was eight, I used to love reading my mum's old nursing textbooks. She trained in the 1930s when we didn't have many of the medical advances we have today. I was excited by the pictures, which were brightly coloured drawings and photographs. Somehow the bright colours heightened the scariness and power of some of the images, which included diseased organs and patients with advanced surgical problems! These pictures inked my imagination and along with my mums' stories of nursing during the Second World War brought me into nursing in the 1970s.

Between my mum's training and mine, a lot had changed. I was lucky to be able to go to Edinburgh University and start my training there. I loved the combination of being a university student and doing practical nursing placements in a wide range of areas. But it was the university side which stuck with me. Somehow, I couldn't resist the pull of research, so I was one of the first nurses to combine working as a nurse with doing research.

I was also lucky to be able to branch out further and go to Oxford University to do my doctorate in history. This may seem a strange path, but it was studying the history of medicine and nursing, and has been very useful for my career. With my research work I've been able to travel the world; work with a lot of very interesting people, including politicians and even prime ministers taking an interest in nursing. I've also worked with some of the top scientists and historians. Looking back, those images in my mum's textbooks have stayed with me – and I have even studied those textbooks as part of my research!

What happens to you when you are eight can have a lasting influence on what you do and who you become, and I hope you may choose nursing and find it as amazing as I do.

Across the Globe

Dr Lissette Aviles, *Lecturer in Nursing Studies*

One of the most fascinating things about nursing is its global nature. Nurses care for people, children, families and communities across the world and regardless of where you are from you can live and work as a nurse by sharing your passion and commitment to helping people's lives.

I grew up in Chile, a long and narrow Spanish-speaking country at the south end of the American continent. Chile has wonderful nature and geography, including the driest desert in the world, the Andes Mountains, volcanoes, the wonderful fiords and Patagonia in the south. As a child I was a Girl Scout and learnt to care for the environment and people to try to make the world a better place. My passion for helping others made me go into nursing.

I remember that from my early years I was both fascinated and

honoured by making people feel better when they were sick or suffering. I learnt that nurses based their practice on science, research and knowledge, work in teams and are committed to helping people's health everywhere in the world. Nursing science inspired me to continue studying and teaching other nurses the art of caring in South America and Europe. Although countries differ in language and culture, caring for people requires the same compassion and love, particularly when they need help.

In 2016, I moved to Scotland to continue my journey of caring, teaching and investigating how to to care for people worldwide. Nurses can practise their passion everywhere! I must tell you that I love my work and I would like to inspire others to follow their dreams. Even if it involves moving across the globe, learning another language and making new family and friends. Now, my home is in Scotland, and I'm so proud of being a global nurse.

Waving in Surgery

Sara Dalby, *Surgical Care Practitioner*

I didn't know I would love the operating theatre – where people have their operations in a hospital – until I had my first placement on an orthopaedic ward and went along to watch a lady have an operation on her hip. I thought it was so interesting watching the surgery and seeing all the different surgical instruments.

After this first experience, I went to work in an operating theatre as a student nurse. After I qualified as a nurse I was the scrub nurse for lots of different pateients, where I had to make sure the surgeon had the instruments and equipment they needed to carry out the operation safely.

As I developed in my job as a nurse, I did extra training. Firstly, I trained to be a surgical assistant. This meant I was still in the operating theatre, but I also helped with the operations by holding a camera for keyhole surgery or holding an instrument to help the surgeon.

I then became a surgical care practitioner. This role meant I could see and talk to the patients to listen to what their problems were, and to help diagnose them. I helped in the operating theatre too, performed minor surgeries myself and looked after patients on the ward after their surgery.

The first surgery I saw was as a student nurse. I saw a lady having a hip replacement. I tried to see what was happening and moved slightly to the left, there was a sheet up and the lady having the surgery waved at me. I didn't realize that people could have surgery but be awake! I have enjoyed all my nursing roles in surgery, there are so many different things you can do, I hope you find my story inspirational!

"You're That School Nurse!"

Sharon White, *CEO School and*
Public Health Nurses Association

I grew up in a very poor household, a child of Irish immigrants who struggled to find decent jobs and were poorly paid. We were allocated damp, cramped housing, which resulted in me experiencing recurrent bronchitis as a child and missing out on lots of school. I realized very early in life that things weren't always fair.

However, my parents were always willing to share what little we had; they became foster carers, parenting a further 100+ vulnerable children, improving their health and, indeed, their life chances and outcomes. I am delighted to have inherited some of their genes – I was, it would seem, forever destined to be a 'carer'.

Following a period as a qualified adult nurse, working in the community as part of my midwifery training was a 'penny drop' and career-defining moment. I realized that I could influence the health of families in a preventative way, promoting and protecting them rather than treating their illnesses in hospital.

With my focus clearly fixed on children, I landed in school nursing and stayed there for over thirty years as a specialist public health nurse.

From singing, dancing, splashing, handwashing, nose-blowing, bottom-wiping, toothbrushing through to listening, empowering, advocating and protecting from abuse and neglect, the role is so very varied and no two days are the same. There are also checks on vision, hearing, healthy lifestyles, poos, wees, through to tackling tantrums, depression, bullying and exam stress.

It's supporting children, young people, parents, carers, schools and more, together aiming for the best health and wellbeing and, importantly, happy children and citizens.

I bumped into Ellie and her two beautiful children recently at a supermarket.

"You're that school nurse who helped me when I was really low and was hurting myself – the only one who really got it! You got me and my brother to a safe place to live," she said.

What's not to like about being a school nurse?

The Buzz

Deborah Sturdy, *Chief Nurse Adult Social Care England*

I t's great being a nurse! You meet so many people and help them get better, stronger and be the best they can be.

You look after their families too and help them through sad times when sometimes, despite best efforts, people don't always get better.

Nurses are important people. They work in our hospitals, schools, communities, in people's homes and in a variety of settings, including care homes. They do good work in many places with lots of people, including babies, children and teenagers. They look after mums and dads, aunties and uncles and grandparents. They look

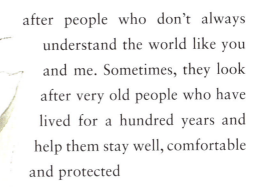

after people who don't always understand the world like you and me. Sometimes, they look after very old people who have lived for a hundred years and help them stay well, comfortable and protected

Being a nurse is a rare and special privilege, because you get to know people from different backgrounds, cultures and who have different experiences. It teaches you to be accepting of everyone and helps you understand the world and the diverse communities within it. Nursing can be fun, some days can make you laugh when you hear the stories people tell you, and some days it can be sad, when those you look after don't get better.

Most of the time, you return home from a long day and, even when you are tired and just want to go to bed, you can take comfort and satisfaction from the fact that you have done something good. Even small actions have huge, positive effects if they make someone feel better. To have that power, the ability to transform lives, is the buzz we get from careers in social care.

Nursing and Midwifery Roles

You'll have seen while reading this book that nursing and midwifery staff work in many different places and have many different jobs to ensure people, their families and communities are well looked after when they are unwell or in need of health advice. You can find nurses and midwives in hospitals, care homes, schools, universities and doctor's surgeries, as well as prisons, the armed forces and even on cruise ships! They might even visit your house to help you or a member of your family.

Nurses and midwives look after everyone – babies, children and young people; adults and elderly people; people who are in urgent need of help and people who have been unwell for a long time. They help people with physical injuries, learning disabilities, mental health challenges and when people are having a baby. They also lead teams of nurses and other health workers and use their skills and knowledge to make important decisions on how best to look after people, to ensure everyone feels safe and cared for. They work closely alongside doctors, too. Nurses and midwives also work in universities to teach and undertake research to help patients and their families to receive the best possible care in the future.

Glossary

accident and emergency – the department in a hospital where people who have severe injuries or sudden illness are taken for emergency treatment

advanced nurse practitioner – a registered nurse who has done extra training to be able to examine, assess, make diagnoses, treat, and prescribe medicine for patients

autism – a lifelong developmental disability which affects how people communicate and interact with the world. If you're autistic, your brain works in a different way from other people.

cardiac – related to the heart

cerebral palsy – the name for a group of lifelong conditions that affect movement and co-ordination. It's caused by a problem with the brain that develops before, during or soon after birth.

clinical – related to the direct observation and treatment of patients

complex care service – a team that looks after patients who need a lot of additional support on a daily basis

Covid – or Covid-19 or coronavirus: an illness with symptoms similar to colds and flu that caused a worldwide pandemic in 2020

degree – a course of study at a university or college, see also *doctorate*

district nurse – nurses who work in the community, rather than in a hospital

doctorate – the highest degree awarded by a university, see also *degree*

emotional intelligence – the ability to understand, use and manage your emotions in positive ways

fertility – the ability to have babies

general practice (GP) – a doctor's surgery where general practitioners (GPs) treat all common medical conditions

healthcare support worker – a term that covers a variety of health and care support roles, including healthcare assistant (HCA), nursing assistant, theatre support worker, maternity support worker and more

HIV/AIDS – HIV (human immunodeficiency virus) is a virus that attacks the body's immune system. If HIV is not treated, it can lead to AIDS (acquired immunodeficiency syndrome)

intensive care unit (ICU) – a special hospital ward that provides treatment and care for people who are very ill; also called 'critical care unit'

learning disability – any of various conditions that cause difficulty in learning a basic skill such as reading or writing; also referred to as a 'special need'

maternity – the help and medical care given to a woman when she is pregnant and when she gives birth

mental health nurse – a nurse who specializes in the care of patients with mental health issues

midwife – someone who provides care and support to women and their families while pregnant, while giving birth and during the period after a baby's birth

NHS (National Health Service) – the medical and healthcare services that everyone living in the UK can use without being asked to pay

operating theatre – a special room in a hospital where surgeons carry out medical operations

orthopaedic – related to people's joints and spines

paediatric – the area of medicine that is concerned with the treatment of children's illnesses

palliative care – if you have an illness that cannot be cured, palliative care makes you as comfortable as possible by managing your pain and other symptoms

physiology – the scientific study of how people's and animals' bodies function, and of how plants function

registered nurse (RN) – any nurse who has completed their training

rehabilitation – 'rehab'; the process of becoming better again after being ill

renal – related to the kidneys

surgery – a medical treatment in which someone's body is cut open so that a doctor can try to repair it

vaccine – a substance used to protect people and animals from very serious diseases

ward – a room in a hospital which has beds for many people

work placement – a temporary job that gives a trainee experience of the job they are training for